The Tragical History of Dr. Faustus

The Tragical History of Dr. Faustus

by Christoper Marlowe

Wilder Publications, LLC.
PO Box 3005
Radford VA 24143-3005

ISBN 10: 1-61720-693-8
ISBN 13: 978-1-61720-693-1

Table of Contents:

DRAMATIS PERSONAE.

THE POPE.
CARDINAL OF LORRAIN.
THE EMPEROR OF GERMANY.
DUKE OF VANHOLT.
FAUSTUS.
VALDES,   ] friends to FAUSTUS.
CORNELIUS,]
WAGNER, servant to FAUSTUS.
Clown.
ROBIN.
RALPH.
Vintner.
Horse-courser.
A Knight.
An Old Man.
Scholars, Friars, and Attendants.
DUCHESS OF VANHOLT
LUCIFER.
BELZEBUB.
MEPHISTOPHILIS.
Good Angel.
Evil Angel.
The Seven Deadly Sins.
Devils.
Spirits in the shapes of ALEXANDER THE GREAT, of his Paramour
    and of HELEN.
Chorus.

The Tragical History of Doctor Faustus from the Quarto of 1604.

Enter CHORUS.

CHORUS. Not marching now in fields of Thrasymene,
Where Mars did mate the Carthaginians;
Nor sporting in the dalliance of love,
In courts of kings where state is overturn'd;
Nor in the pomp of proud audacious deeds,
Intends our Muse to vaunt her heavenly verse:
Only this, gentlemen,—we must perform
The form of Faustus' fortunes, good or bad:
To patient judgments we appeal our plaud,
And speak for Faustus in his infancy.
Now is he born, his parents base of stock,
In Germany, within a town call'd Rhodes:
Of riper years, to Wertenberg he went,
Whereas his kinsmen chiefly brought him up.
So soon he profits in divinity,
The fruitful plot of scholarism grac'd,
That shortly he was grac'd with doctor's name,
Excelling all whose sweet delight disputes
In heavenly matters of theology;
Till swoln with cunning, of a self-conceit,
His waxen wings did mount above his reach,
And, melting, heavens conspir'd his overthrow;
For, falling to a devilish exercise,
And glutted now with learning's golden gifts,
He surfeits upon cursed necromancy;
Nothing so sweet as magic is to him,
Which he prefers before his chiefest bliss:
And this the man that in his study sits.
[Exit.]

FAUSTUS discovered in his study.

FAUSTUS. Settle thy studies, Faustus, and begin
To sound the depth of that thou wilt profess:

Having commenc'd, be a divine in shew,
Yet level at the end of every art,
And live and die in Aristotle's works.
Sweet Analytics, 'tis thou hast ravish'd me!
Bene disserere est finis logices.
Is, to dispute well, logic's chiefest end?
Affords this art no greater miracle?
Then read no more; thou hast attain'd that end:
A greater subject fitteth Faustus' wit:
Bid Economy farewell, and Galen come,
Seeing, Ubi desinit philosophus, ibi incipit medicus:
Be a physician, Faustus; heap up gold,
And be eterniz'd for some wondrous cure:
Summum bonum medicinae sanitas,
The end of physic is our body's health.
Why, Faustus, hast thou not attain'd that end?
Is not thy common talk found aphorisms?
Are not thy bills hung up as monuments,
Whereby whole cities have escap'd the plague,
And thousand desperate maladies been eas'd?
Yet art thou still but Faustus, and a man.
Couldst thou make men to live eternally,
Or, being dead, raise them to life again,
Then this profession were to be esteem'd.
Physic, farewell! Where is Justinian?
    [Reads.]
Si una eademque res legatur duobus, alter rem,
alter valorem rei, &c.
    A pretty case of paltry legacies!
    [Reads.]
Exhoereditare filium non potest pater, nisi, &c.
    Such is the subject of the institute,
And universal body of the law:
This study fits a mercenary drudge,
Who aims at nothing but external trash;
Too servile and illiberal for me.
When all is done, divinity is best:
Jerome's Bible, Faustus; view it well.
    [Reads.]

Stipendium peccati mors est.
                         Ha!
                                Stipendium, &c.
    The reward of sin is death: that's hard.
        [Reads.]
Si peccasse negamus, fallimur, et nulla est in nobis veritas;
    If we say that we have no sin, we deceive ourselves, and
there's no truth in us. Why, then, belike we must sin, and so
consequently die:
Ay, we must die an everlasting death.
What doctrine call you this, Che sera, sera,
What will be, shall be? Divinity, adieu!
These metaphysics of magicians,
And necromantic books are heavenly;
Lines, circles, scenes, letters, and characters;
Ay, these are those that Faustus most desires.
O, what a world of profit and delight,
Of power, of honour, of omnipotence,
Is promis'd to the studious artizan!
All things that move between the quiet poles
Shall be at my command: emperors and kings
Are but obeyed in their several provinces,
Nor can they raise the wind, or rend the clouds;
But his dominion that exceeds in this,
Stretcheth as far as doth the mind of man;
A sound magician is a mighty god:
Here, Faustus, tire thy brains to gain a deity.
        Enter WAGNER.
    Wagner, commend me to my dearest friends,
The German Valdes and Cornelius;
Request them earnestly to visit me.
    WAGNER. I will, sir.
    [Exit.]
    FAUSTUS. Their conference will be a greater help to me
Than all my labours, plod I ne'er so fast.
        Enter GOOD ANGEL and EVIL ANGEL.
    GOOD ANGEL. O, Faustus, lay that damned book aside,
And gaze not on it, lest it tempt thy soul,
And heap God's heavy wrath upon thy head!

Read, read the Scriptures:—that is blasphemy.

EVIL ANGEL. Go forward, Faustus, in that famous art
Wherein all Nature's treasure is contain'd:
Be thou on earth as Jove is in the sky,
Lord and commander of these elements.

[Exeunt Angels.]

FAUSTUS. How am I glutted with conceit of this!
Shall I make spirits fetch me what I please,
Resolve me of all ambiguities,
Perform what desperate enterprise I will?
I'll have them fly to India for gold,
Ransack the ocean for orient pearl,
And search all corners of the new-found world
For pleasant fruits and princely delicates;
I'll have them read me strange philosophy,
And tell the secrets of all foreign kings;
I'll have them wall all Germany with brass,
And make swift Rhine circle fair Wertenberg;
I'll have them fill the public schools with silk,
Wherewith the students shall be bravely clad;
I'll levy soldiers with the coin they bring,
And chase the Prince of Parma from our land,
And reign sole king of all the provinces;
Yea, stranger engines for the brunt of war,
Than was the fiery keel at Antwerp's bridge,
I'll make my servile spirits to invent.

Enter VALDES and CORNELIUS.

Come, German Valdes, and Cornelius,
And make me blest with your sage conference.
Valdes, sweet Valdes, and Cornelius,
Know that your words have won me at the last
To practice magic and concealed arts:
Yet not your words only, but mine own fantasy,
That will receive no object; for my head
But ruminates on necromantic skill.
Philosophy is odious and obscure;
Both law and physic are for petty wits;
Divinity is basest of the three,
Unpleasant, harsh, contemptible, and vile:

'Tis magic, magic, that hath ravish'd me.
Then, gentle friends, aid me in this attempt;
And I, that have with concise syllogisms
Gravell'd the pastors of the German church,
And made the flowering pride of Wertenberg
Swarm to my problems, as the infernal spirits
On sweet Musaeus when he came to hell,
Will be as cunning as Agrippa was,
Whose shadow made all Europe honour him.
  VALDES. Faustus, these books, thy wit, and our experience,
Shall make all nations to canonize us.
As Indian Moors obey their Spanish lords,
So shall the spirits of every element
Be always serviceable to us three;
Like lions shall they guard us when we please;
Like Almain rutters with their horsemen's staves,
Or Lapland giants, trotting by our sides;
Sometimes like women, or unwedded maids,
Shadowing more beauty in their airy brows
Than have the white breasts of the queen of love:
From Venice shall they drag huge argosies,
And from America the golden fleece
That yearly stuffs old Philip's treasury;
If learned Faustus will be resolute.
  FAUSTUS. Valdes, as resolute am I in this
As thou to live: therefore object it not.
  CORNELIUS. The miracles that magic will perform
Will make thee vow to study nothing else.
He that is grounded in astrology,
Enrich'd with tongues, well seen in minerals,
Hath all the principles magic doth require:
Then doubt not, Faustus, but to be renowm'd,
And more frequented for this mystery
Than heretofore the Delphian oracle.
The spirits tell me they can dry the sea,
And fetch the treasure of all foreign wrecks,
Ay, all the wealth that our forefathers hid
Within the massy entrails of the earth:
Then tell me, Faustus, what shall we three want?

FAUSTUS. Nothing, Cornelius. O, this cheers my soul!
Come, shew me some demonstrations magical,
That I may conjure in some lusty grove,
And have these joys in full possession.

VALDES. Then haste thee to some solitary grove,
And bear wise Bacon's and Albertus' works,
The Hebrew Psalter, and New Testament;
And whatsoever else is requisite
We will inform thee ere our conference cease.

CORNELIUS. Valdes, first let him know the words of art;
And then, all other ceremonies learn'd,
Faustus may try his cunning by himself.

VALDES. First I'll instruct thee in the rudiments,
And then wilt thou be perfecter than I.

FAUSTUS. Then come and dine with me, and, after meat,
We'll canvass every quiddity thereof;
For, ere I sleep, I'll try what I can do:
This night I'll conjure, though I die therefore.

   [Exeunt.]

      Enter two SCHOLARS.

FIRST SCHOLAR. I wonder what's become of Faustus, that was wont
to make our schools ring with sic probo.

SECOND SCHOLAR. That shall we know, for see, here comes his boy.

      Enter WAGNER.

FIRST SCHOLAR. How now, sirrah! where's thy master?

WAGNER. God in heaven knows.

SECOND SCHOLAR. Why, dost not thou know?

WAGNER. Yes, I know; but that follows not.

FIRST SCHOLAR. Go to, sirrah! leave your jesting, and tell us
where he is.

WAGNER. That follows not necessary by force of argument, that you,
being licentiates, should stand upon: therefore acknowledge
your error, and be attentive.

SECOND SCHOLAR. Why, didst thou not say thou knewest?

WAGNER. Have you any witness on't?

FIRST SCHOLAR. Yes, sirrah, I heard you.

WAGNER. Ask my fellow if I be a thief.

SECOND SCHOLAR. Well, you will not tell us?

WAGNER. Yes, sir, I will tell you: yet, if you were not dunces,

you would never ask me such a question; for is not he corpus
naturale? and is not that mobile? then wherefore should you
ask me such a question? But that I am by nature phlegmatic,
slow to wrath, and prone to lechery (to love, I would say),
it were not for you to come within forty foot of the place
of execution, although I do not doubt to see you both hanged
the next sessions. Thus having triumphed over you, I will set
my countenance like a precisian, and begin to speak thus:—
Truly, my dear brethren, my master is within at dinner,
with Valdes and Cornelius, as this wine, if it could speak,
would inform your worships: and so, the Lord bless you,
preserve you, and keep you, my dear brethren, my dear brethren!
   [Exit.]

   FIRST SCHOLAR. Nay, then, I fear he is fallen into that damned art
for which they two are infamous through the world.

   SECOND SCHOLAR. Were he a stranger, and not allied to me, yet
should
I grieve for him. But, come, let us go and inform the Rector,
and see if he by his grave counsel can reclaim him.

   FIRST SCHOLAR. O, but I fear me nothing can reclaim him!

   SECOND SCHOLAR. Yet let us try what we can do.
   [Exeunt.]

     Enter FAUSTUS to conjure.

   FAUSTUS. Now that the gloomy shadow of the earth,
Longing to view Orion's drizzling look,
Leaps from th' antartic world unto the sky,
And dims the welkin with her pitchy breath,
Faustus, begin thine incantations,
And try if devils will obey thy hest,
Seeing thou hast pray'd and sacrific'd to them.
Within this circle is Jehovah's name,
Forward and backward anagrammatiz'd,
Th' abbreviated names of holy saints,
Figures of every adjunct to the heavens,
And characters of signs and erring stars,
By which the spirits are enforc'd to rise:
Then fear not, Faustus, but be resolute,
And try the uttermost magic can perform.—
Sint mihi dei Acherontis propitii! Valeat numen triplex Jehovoe!

Ignei, aerii, aquatani spiritus, salvete! Orientis princeps
Belzebub, inferni ardentis monarcha, et Demogorgon, propitiamus
vos, ut appareat et surgat Mephistophilis, quod tumeraris:
per Jehovam, Gehennam, et consecratam aquam quam nunc spargo,
signumque crucis quod nunc facio, et per vota nostra, ipse nunc
surgat nobis dicatus Mephistophilis!

     Enter MEPHISTOPHILIS.

  I charge thee to return, and change thy shape;
Thou art too ugly to attend on me:
Go, and return an old Franciscan friar;
That holy shape becomes a devil best.

   [Exit MEPHISTOPHILIS.]

  I see there's virtue in my heavenly words:
Who would not be proficient in this art?
How pliant is this Mephistophilis,
Full of obedience and humility!
Such is the force of magic and my spells:
No, Faustus, thou art conjuror laureat,
That canst command great Mephistophilis:
Quin regis Mephistophilis fratris imagine.

     Re-enter MEPHISTOPHILIS like a Franciscan friar.

  MEPHIST. Now, Faustus, what wouldst thou have me do?

  FAUSTUS. I charge thee wait upon me whilst I live,
To do whatever Faustus shall command,
Be it to make the moon drop from her sphere,
Or the ocean to overwhelm the world.

  MEPHIST. I am a servant to great Lucifer,
And may not follow thee without his leave:
No more than he commands must we perform.

  FAUSTUS. Did not he charge thee to appear to me?

  MEPHIST. No, I came hither of mine own accord.

  FAUSTUS. Did not my conjuring speeches raise thee? speak.

  MEPHIST. That was the cause, but yet per accidens;
For, when we hear one rack the name of God,
Abjure the Scriptures and his Saviour Christ,
We fly, in hope to get his glorious soul;
Nor will we come, unless he use such means
Whereby he is in danger to be damn'd.
Therefore the shortest cut for conjuring

Is stoutly to abjure the Trinity,
And pray devoutly to the prince of hell.
    FAUSTUS. So Faustus hath
Already done; and holds this principle,
There is no chief but only Belzebub;
To whom Faustus doth dedicate himself.
This word "damnation" terrifies not him,
For he confounds hell in Elysium:
His ghost be with the old philosophers!
But, leaving these vain trifles of men's souls,
Tell me what is that Lucifer thy lord?
    MEPHIST. Arch-regent and commander of all spirits.
    FAUSTUS. Was not that Lucifer an angel once?
    MEPHIST. Yes, Faustus, and most dearly lov'd of God.
    FAUSTUS. How comes it, then, that he is prince of devils?
    MEPHIST. O, by aspiring pride and insolence;
For which God threw him from the face of heaven.
    FAUSTUS. And what are you that live with Lucifer?
    MEPHIST. Unhappy spirits that fell with Lucifer,
Conspir'd against our God with Lucifer,
And are for ever damn'd with Lucifer.
    FAUSTUS. Where are you damn'd?
    MEPHIST. In hell.
    FAUSTUS. How comes it, then, that thou art out of hell?
    MEPHIST. Why, this is hell, nor am I out of it:
Think'st thou that I, who saw the face of God,
And tasted the eternal joys of heaven,
Am not tormented with ten thousand hells,
In being depriv'd of everlasting bliss?
O, Faustus, leave these frivolous demands,
Which strike a terror to my fainting soul!
    FAUSTUS. What, is great Mephistophilis so passionate
For being deprived of the joys of heaven?
Learn thou of Faustus manly fortitude,
And scorn those joys thou never shalt possess.
Go bear these tidings to great Lucifer:
Seeing Faustus hath incurr'd eternal death
By desperate thoughts against Jove's deity,
Say, he surrenders up to him his soul,

So he will spare him four and twenty years,
Letting him live in all voluptuousness;
Having thee ever to attend on me,
To give me whatsoever I shall ask,
To tell me whatsoever I demand,
To slay mine enemies, and aid my friends,
And always be obedient to my will.
Go and return to mighty Lucifer,
And meet me in my study at midnight,
And then resolve me of thy master's mind.
  MEPHIST. I will, Faustus.
  [Exit.]
  FAUSTUS. Had I as many souls as there be stars,
I'd give them all for Mephistophilis.
By him I'll be great emperor of the world,
And make a bridge thorough the moving air,
To pass the ocean with a band of men;
I'll join the hills that bind the Afric shore,
And make that country continent to Spain,
And both contributory to my crown:
The Emperor shall not live but by my leave,
Nor any potentate of Germany.
Now that I have obtain'd what I desir'd,
I'll live in speculation of this art,
Till Mephistophilis return again.
  [Exit.]
    Enter WAGNER and CLOWN.
  WAGNER. Sirrah boy, come hither.
  CLOWN. How, boy! swowns, boy! I hope you have seen many boys
with such pickadevaunts as I have: boy, quotha!
  WAGNER. Tell me, sirrah, hast thou any comings in?
  CLOWN. Ay, and goings out too; you may see else.
  WAGNER. Alas, poor slave! see how poverty jesteth in his nakedness!
the villain is bare and out of service, and so hungry, that I know
he would give his soul to the devil for a shoulder of mutton,
though it were blood-raw.
  CLOWN. How! my soul to the devil for a shoulder of mutton, though
'twere blood-raw! not so, good friend: by'r lady, I had need
have it well roasted, and good sauce to it, if I pay so dear.

WAGNER. Well, wilt thou serve me, and I'll make thee go like Qui mihi discipulus?

CLOWN. How, in verse?

WAGNER. No, sirrah; in beaten silk and staves-acre.

CLOWN. How, how, knaves-acre! ay, I thought that was all the land his father left him. Do you hear? I would be sorry to rob you of your living.

WAGNER. Sirrah, I say in staves-acre.

CLOWN. Oho, oho, staves-acre! why, then, belike, if I were your man, I should be full of vermin.

WAGNER. So thou shalt, whether thou beest with me or no. But, sirrah, leave your jesting, and bind yourself presently unto me for seven years, or I'll turn all the lice about thee into familiars, and they shall tear thee in pieces.

CLOWN. Do you hear, sir? you may save that labour; they are too familiar with me already: swowns, they are as bold with my flesh as if they had paid for their meat and drink.

WAGNER. Well, do you hear, sirrah? hold, take these guilders.

[Gives money.]

CLOWN. Gridirons! what be they?

WAGNER. Why, French crowns.

CLOWN. Mass, but for the name of French crowns, a man were as good have as many English counters. And what should I do with these?

WAGNER. Why, now, sirrah, thou art at an hour's warning, whensoever or wheresoever the devil shall fetch thee.

CLOWN. No, no; here, take your gridirons again.

WAGNER. Truly, I'll none of them.

CLOWN. Truly, but you shall.

WAGNER. Bear witness I gave them him.

CLOWN. Bear witness I give them you again.

WAGNER. Well, I will cause two devils presently to fetch thee away.—Baliol and Belcher!

CLOWN. Let your Baliol and your Belcher come here, and I'll knock them, they were never so knocked since they were devils: say I should kill one of them, what would folks say? "Do ye see yonder tall fellow in the round slop? he has killed the devil." So I should be called Kill-devil all the parish over.

Enter two DEVILS; and the CLOWN runs up and down crying.

WAGNER. Baliol and Belcher,—spirits, away!

[Exeunt DEVILS.]

CLOWN. What, are they gone? a vengeance on them! they have vile
long nails. There was a he-devil and a she-devil: I'll tell you
how you shall know them; all he-devils has horns, and all
she-devils has clifts and cloven feet.

WAGNER. Well, sirrah, follow me.

CLOWN. But, do you hear? if I should serve you, would you teach
me to raise up Banios and Belcheos?

WAGNER. I will teach thee to turn thyself to any thing, to a dog,
or a cat, or a mouse, or a rat, or any thing.

CLOWN. How! a Christian fellow to a dog, or a cat, a mouse,
or a rat! no, no, sir; if you turn me into any thing, let it be
in the likeness of a little pretty frisking flea, that I may be
here and there and every where: O, I'll tickle the pretty wenches'
plackets! I'll be amongst them, i'faith.

WAGNER. Well, sirrah, come.

CLOWN. But, do you hear, Wagner?

WAGNER. How!—Baliol and Belcher!

CLOWN. O Lord! I pray, sir, let Banio and Belcher go sleep.

WAGNER. Villain, call me Master Wagner, and let thy left eye be
diametarily fixed upon my right heel, with quasi vestigiis
nostris insistere.

[Exit.]

CLOWN. God forgive me, he speaks Dutch fustian. Well, I'll follow
him; I'll serve him, that's flat.

[Exit.]

FAUSTUS discovered in his study.

FAUSTUS. Now, Faustus, must
Thou needs be damn'd, and canst thou not be sav'd:
What boots it, then, to think of God or heaven?
Away with such vain fancies, and despair;
Despair in God, and trust in Belzebub:
Now go not backward; no, Faustus, be resolute:
Why waver'st thou? O, something soundeth in mine ears,
"Abjure this magic, turn to God again!"
Ay, and Faustus will turn to God again.
To God? he loves thee not;

The god thou serv'st is thine own appetite,
Wherein is fix'd the love of Belzebub:
To him I'll build an altar and a church,
And offer lukewarm blood of new-born babes.

      Enter GOOD ANGEL and EVIL ANGEL.

  GOOD ANGEL. Sweet Faustus, leave that execrable art.

  FAUSTUS. Contrition, prayer, repentance—what of them?

  GOOD ANGEL. O, they are means to bring thee unto heaven!

  EVIL ANGEL. Rather illusions, fruits of lunacy,
That make men foolish that do trust them most.

  GOOD ANGEL. Sweet Faustus, think of heaven and heavenly things.

  EVIL ANGEL. No, Faustus; think of honour and of wealth.

  [Exeunt ANGELS.]

  FAUSTUS. Of wealth!
Why, the signiory of Embden shall be mine.
When Mephistophilis shall stand by me,
What god can hurt thee, Faustus? thou art safe
Cast no more doubts.—Come, Mephistophilis,
And bring glad tidings from great Lucifer;—
Is't not midnight?—come, Mephistophilis,
Veni, veni, Mephistophile!

      Enter MEPHISTOPHILIS.

  Now tell me what says Lucifer, thy lord?

  MEPHIST. That I shall wait on Faustus whilst he lives,
So he will buy my service with his soul.

  FAUSTUS. Already Faustus hath hazarded that for thee.

  MEPHIST. But, Faustus, thou must bequeath it solemnly,
And write a deed of gift with thine own blood;
For that security craves great Lucifer.
If thou deny it, I will back to hell.

  FAUSTUS. Stay, Mephistophilis, and tell me, what good will my soul
do thy lord?

  MEPHIST. Enlarge his kingdom.

  FAUSTUS. Is that the reason why he tempts us thus?

  MEPHIST. Solamen miseris socios habuisse doloris.

  FAUSTUS. Why, have you any pain that torture others!

  MEPHIST. As great as have the human souls of men.
But, tell me, Faustus, shall I have thy soul?
And I will be thy slave, and wait on thee,

And give thee more than thou hast wit to ask.

    FAUSTUS. Ay, Mephistophilis, I give it thee.

    MEPHIST. Then, Faustus, stab thine arm courageously,
And bind thy soul, that at some certain day
Great Lucifer may claim it as his own;
And then be thou as great as Lucifer.

    FAUSTUS. [Stabbing his arm] Lo, Mephistophilis, for love of thee,
I cut mine arm, and with my proper blood
Assure my soul to be great Lucifer's,
Chief lord and regent of perpetual night!
View here the blood that trickles from mine arm,
And let it be propitious for my wish.

    MEPHIST. But, Faustus, thou must
Write it in manner of a deed of gift.

    FAUSTUS. Ay, so I will [Writes]. But, Mephistophilis,
My blood congeals, and I can write no more.

    MEPHIST. I'll fetch thee fire to dissolve it straight.
    [Exit.]

    FAUSTUS. What might the staying of my blood portend?
Is it unwilling I should write this bill?
Why streams it not, that I may write afresh?
FAUSTUS GIVES TO THEE HIS SOUL: ah, there it stay'd!
Why shouldst thou not? is not thy soul shine own?
Then write again, FAUSTUS GIVES TO THEE HIS SOUL.

        Re-enter MEPHISTOPHILIS with a chafer of coals.

    MEPHIST. Here's fire; come, Faustus, set it on.

    FAUSTUS. So, now the blood begins to clear again;
Now will I make an end immediately.
    [Writes.]

    MEPHIST. O, what will not I do to obtain his soul?
    [Aside.]

    FAUSTUS. Consummatum est; this bill is ended,
And Faustus hath bequeath'd his soul to Lucifer.
But what is this inscription on mine arm?
Homo, fuge: whither should I fly?
If unto God, he'll throw me down to hell.
My senses are deceiv'd; here's nothing writ:—
I see it plain; here in this place is writ,
Homo, fuge: yet shall not Faustus fly.

MEPHIST. I'll fetch him somewhat to delight his mind.
[Aside, and then exit.]
   Re-enter MEPHISTOPHILIS with DEVILS, who give crowns
and rich apparel to FAUSTUS, dance, and then depart.
FAUSTUS. Speak, Mephistophilis, what means this show?
MEPHIST. Nothing, Faustus, but to delight thy mind withal,
And to shew thee what magic can perform.
FAUSTUS. But may I raise up spirits when I please?
MEPHIST. Ay, Faustus, and do greater things than these.
FAUSTUS. Then there's enough for a thousand souls.
Here, Mephistophilis, receive this scroll,
A deed of gift of body and of soul:
But yet conditionally that thou perform
All articles prescrib'd between us both.
MEPHIST. Faustus, I swear by hell and Lucifer
To effect all promises between us made!
FAUSTUS. Then hear me read them. [Reads] ON THESE CONDI-
TIONS
   FOLLOWING. FIRST, THAT FAUSTUS MAY BE A SPIRIT IN
FORM AND
   SUBSTANCE. SECONDLY, THAT MEPHISTOPHILIS SHALL BE
HIS SERVANT,
   AND AT HIS COMMAND. THIRDLY, THAT MEPHISTOPHILIS
SHALL DO FOR HIM,
   AND BRING HIM WHATSOEVER HE DESIRES. FOURTHLY,
THAT HE SHALL
   BE IN HIS CHAMBER OR HOUSE INVISIBLE. LASTLY, THAT HE
SHALL APPEAR
   TO THE SAID JOHN FAUSTUS, AT ALL TIMES, IN WHAT FORM
OR SHAPE
   SOEVER HE PLEASE. I, JOHN FAUSTUS, OF WERTENBERG,
DOCTOR, BY
   THESE PRESENTS, DO GIVE BOTH BODY AND SOUL TO
LUCIFER PRINCE OF
   THE EAST, AND HIS MINISTER MEPHISTOPHILIS; AND FUR-
THERMORE GRANT
   UNTO THEM, THAT, TWENTY-FOUR YEARS BEING EXPIRED,
THE ARTICLES

ABOVE-WRITTEN INVIOLATE, FULL POWER TO FETCH OR
CARRY THE SAID

JOHN FAUSTUS, BODY AND SOUL, FLESH, BLOOD, OR GOODS,
INTO THEIR

HABITATION WHERESOEVER. BY ME, JOHN FAUSTUS.

MEPHIST. Speak, Faustus, do you deliver this as your deed?

FAUSTUS. Ay, take it, and the devil give thee good on't!

MEPHIST. Now, Faustus, ask what thou wilt.

FAUSTUS. First will I question with thee about hell.
Tell me, where is the place that men call hell?

MEPHIST. Under the heavens.

FAUSTUS. Ay, but whereabout?

MEPHIST. Within the bowels of these elements,
Where we are tortur'd and remain for ever:
Hell hath no limits, nor is circumscrib'd
In one self place; for where we are is hell,
And where hell is, there must we ever be:
And, to conclude, when all the world dissolves,
And every creature shall be purified,
All places shall be hell that are not heaven.

FAUSTUS. Come, I think hell's a fable.

MEPHIST. Ay, think so still, till experience change thy mind.

FAUSTUS. Why, think'st thou, then, that Faustus shall be damn'd?

MEPHIST. Ay, of necessity, for here's the scroll
Wherein thou hast given thy soul to Lucifer.

FAUSTUS. Ay, and body too: but what of that?
Think'st thou that Faustus is so fond to imagine
That, after this life, there is any pain?
Tush, these are trifles and mere old wives' tales.

MEPHIST. But, Faustus, I am an instance to prove the contrary,
For I am damn'd, and am now in hell.

FAUSTUS. How! now in hell!
Nay, an this be hell, I'll willingly be damn'd here:
What! walking, disputing, &c.
But, leaving off this, let me have a wife,
The fairest maid in Germany;
For I am wanton and lascivious,
And cannot live without a wife.

MEPHIST. How! a wife!

I prithee, Faustus, talk not of a wife.

FAUSTUS. Nay, sweet Mephistophilis, fetch me one, for I will have
one.

MEPHIST. Well, thou wilt have one? Sit there till I come: I'll
fetch thee a wife in the devil's name.

  [Exit.]

   Re-enter MEPHISTOPHILIS with a DEVIL drest like a WOMAN,
  with fire-works.

MEPHIST. Tell me, Faustus, how dost thou like thy wife?

FAUSTUS. A plague on her for a hot whore!

MEPHIST. Tut, Faustus,
Marriage is but a ceremonial toy;
If thou lovest me, think no more of it.
I'll cull thee out the fairest courtezans,
And bring them every morning to thy bed:
She whom thine eye shall like, thy heart shall have,
Be she as chaste as was Penelope,
As wise as Saba, or as beautiful
As was bright Lucifer before his fall.
Hold, take this book, peruse it thoroughly:

  [Gives book.]

  The iterating of these lines brings gold;
The framing of this circle on the ground
Brings whirlwinds, tempests, thunder, and lightning;
Pronounce this thrice devoutly to thyself,
And men in armour shall appear to thee,
Ready to execute what thou desir'st.

FAUSTUS. Thanks, Mephistophilis: yet fain would I have a book
wherein I might behold all spells and incantations, that I
might raise up spirits when I please.

MEPHIST. Here they are in this book.

  [Turns to them.]

FAUSTUS. Now would I have a book where I might see all characters
and planets of the heavens, that I might know their motions and
dispositions.

MEPHIST. Here they are too.

  [Turns to them.]

  FAUSTUS. Nay, let me have one book more,—and then I have
done,—

wherein I might see all plants, herbs, and trees, that grow upon
the earth.

MEPHIST. Here they be.

FAUSTUS. O, thou art deceived.

MEPHIST. Tut, I warrant thee.

[Turns to them.]

FAUSTUS. When I behold the heavens, then I repent,
And curse thee, wicked Mephistophilis,
Because thou hast depriv'd me of those joys.

MEPHIST. Why, Faustus,
Thinkest thou heaven is such a glorious thing?
I tell thee, 'tis not half so fair as thou,
Or any man that breathes on earth.

FAUSTUS. How prov'st thou that?

MEPHIST. 'Twas made for man, therefore is man more excellent.

FAUSTUS. If it were made for man, 'twas made for me:
I will renounce this magic and repent.

Enter GOOD ANGEL and EVIL ANGEL.

GOOD ANGEL. Faustus, repent; yet God will pity thee.

EVIL ANGEL. Thou art a spirit; God cannot pity thee.

FAUSTUS. Who buzzeth in mine ears I am a spirit?
Be I a devil, yet God may pity me;
Ay, God will pity me, if I repent.

EVIL ANGEL. Ay, but Faustus never shall repent.

[Exeunt ANGELS.]

FAUSTUS. My heart's so harden'd, I cannot repent:
Scarce can I name salvation, faith, or heaven,
But fearful echoes thunder in mine ears,
"Faustus, thou art damn'd!" then swords, and knives,
Poison, guns, halters, and envenom'd steel
Are laid before me to despatch myself;
And long ere this I should have slain myself,
Had not sweet pleasure conquer'd deep despair.
Have not I made blind Homer sing to me
Of Alexander's love and Oenon's death?
And hath not he, that built the walls of Thebes
With ravishing sound of his melodious harp,
Made music with my Mephistophilis?
Why should I die, then, or basely despair?

I am resolv'd; Faustus shall ne'er repent.—
Come, Mephistophilis, let us dispute again,
And argue of divine astrology.
Tell me, are there many heavens above the moon
Are all celestial bodies but one globe,
As is the substance of this centric earth?
　　MEPHIST. As are the elements, such are the spheres,
Mutually folded in each other's orb,
And, Faustus,
All jointly move upon one axletree,
Whose terminine is term'd the world's wide pole;
Nor are the names of Saturn, Mars, or Jupiter
Feign'd, but are erring stars.
　　FAUSTUS. But, tell me, have they all one motion, both situ et
tempore?
　　MEPHIST. All jointly move from east to west in twenty-four hours
upon the poles of the world; but differ in their motion upon
the poles of the zodiac.
　　FAUSTUS. Tush,
These slender trifles Wagner can decide:
Hath Mephistophilis no greater skill?
Who knows not the double motion of the planets?
The first is finish'd in a natural day;
The second thus; as Saturn in thirty years; Jupiter in twelve;
Mars in four; the Sun, Venus, and Mercury in a year; the Moon in
twenty-eight days. Tush, these are freshmen's suppositions.
But, tell me, hath every sphere a dominion or intelligentia?
　　MEPHIST. Ay.
　　FAUSTUS. How many heavens or spheres are there?
　　MEPHIST. Nine; the seven planets, the firmament, and the empyreal
heaven.
　　FAUSTUS. Well, resolve me in this question; why have we not
conjunctions, oppositions, aspects, eclipses, all at one time,
but in some years we have more, in some less?
　　MEPHIST. Per inoequalem motum respectu totius.
　　FAUSTUS. Well, I am answered. Tell me who made the world?
　　MEPHIST. I will not.
　　FAUSTUS. Sweet Mephistophilis, tell me.
　　MEPHIST. Move me not, for I will not tell thee.

FAUSTUS. Villain, have I not bound thee to tell me any thing?

MEPHIST. Ay, that is not against our kingdom; but this is. Think thou on hell, Faustus, for thou art damned.

FAUSTUS. Think, Faustus, upon God that made the world.

MEPHIST. Remember this.

[Exit.]

FAUSTUS. Ay, go, accursed spirit, to ugly hell!
'Tis thou hast damn'd distressed Faustus' soul.
Is't not too late?

Re-enter GOOD ANGEL and EVIL ANGEL.

EVIL ANGEL. Too late.

GOOD ANGEL. Never too late, if Faustus can repent.

EVIL ANGEL. If thou repent, devils shall tear thee in pieces.

GOOD ANGEL. Repent, and they shall never raze thy skin.

[Exeunt ANGELS.]

FAUSTUS. Ah, Christ, my Saviour,
Seek to save distressed Faustus' soul!

Enter LUCIFER, BELZEBUB, and MEPHISTOPHILIS.

LUCIFER. Christ cannot save thy soul, for he is just:
There's none but I have interest in the same.

FAUSTUS. O, who art thou that look'st so terrible?

LUCIFER. I am Lucifer,
And this is my companion-prince in hell.

FAUSTUS. O, Faustus, they are come to fetch away thy soul!

LUCIFER. We come to tell thee thou dost injure us;
Thou talk'st of Christ, contrary to thy promise:
Thou shouldst not think of God: think of the devil,
And of his dam too.

FAUSTUS. Nor will I henceforth: pardon me in this,
And Faustus vows never to look to heaven,
Never to name God, or to pray to him,
To burn his Scriptures, slay his ministers,
And make my spirits pull his churches down.

LUCIFER. Do so, and we will highly gratify thee. Faustus, we are come from hell to shew thee some pastime: sit down, and thou shalt see all the Seven Deadly Sins appear in their proper shapes.

FAUSTUS. That sight will be as pleasing unto me,
As Paradise was to Adam, the first day
Of his creation.

LUCIFER. Talk not of Paradise nor creation; but mark this show:
talk of the devil, and nothing else.—Come away!

Enter the SEVEN DEADLY SINS.

Now, Faustus, examine them of their several names and dispositions.

FAUSTUS. What art thou, the first?

PRIDE. I am Pride. I disdain to have any parents. I am like to
Ovid's flea; I can creep into every corner of a wench; sometimes,
like a perriwig, I sit upon her brow; or, like a fan of feathers,
I kiss her lips; indeed, I do—what do I not? But, fie, what a
scent is here! I'll not speak another word, except the ground
were perfumed, and covered with cloth of arras.

FAUSTUS. What art thou, the second?

COVETOUSNESS. I am Covetousness, begotten of an old churl, in an
old leathern bag: and, might I have my wish, I would desire that
this house and all the people in it were turned to gold, that I
might lock you up in my good chest: O, my sweet gold!

FAUSTUS. What art thou, the third?

WRATH. I am Wrath. I had neither father nor mother: I leapt out
of a lion's mouth when I was scarce half-an-hour old; and ever
since I have run up and down the world with this case
of rapiers, wounding myself when I had nobody to fight withal.
I was born in hell; and look to it, for some of you shall be
my father.

FAUSTUS. What art thou, the fourth?

ENVY. I am Envy, begotten of a chimney-sweeper and an oyster-wife.
I cannot read, and therefore wish all books were burnt. I am lean
with seeing others eat. O, that there would come a famine through
all the world, that all might die, and I live alone! then thou
shouldst see how fat I would be. But must thou sit, and I stand?
come down, with a vengeance!

FAUSTUS. Away, envious rascal!—What art thou, the fifth?

GLUTTONY. Who I, sir? I am Gluttony. My parents are all dead,
and the devil a penny they have left me, but a bare pension, and
that is thirty meals a-day and ten bevers,—a small trifle
to suffice nature. O, I come of a royal parentage! my grandfather
was a Gammon of Bacon, my grandmother a Hogshead of Claret-wine;
my godfathers were these, Peter Pickle-herring and Martin
Martlemas-beef; O, but my godmother, she was a jolly gentlewoman,
and well-beloved in every good town and city; her name was Mistress

Margery March-beer. Now, Faustus, thou hast heard all my progeny;
wilt thou bid me to supper?

FAUSTUS. No, I'll see thee hanged: thou wilt eat up all my victuals.

GLUTTONY. Then the devil choke thee!

FAUSTUS. Choke thyself, glutton!—What art thou, the sixth?

SLOTH. I am Sloth. I was begotten on a sunny bank, where I have
lain ever since; and you have done me great injury to bring me
from thence: let me be carried thither again by Gluttony and
Lechery. I'll not speak another word for a king's ransom.

FAUSTUS. What are you, Mistress Minx, the seventh and last?

LECHERY. Who I, sir? I am one that loves an inch of raw mutton
better than an ell of fried stock-fish; and the first letter
of my name begins with L.

FAUSTUS. Away, to hell, to hell!

 [Exeunt the SINS.]

LUCIFER. Now, Faustus, how dost thou like this?

FAUSTUS. O, this feeds my soul!

LUCIFER. Tut, Faustus, in hell is all manner of delight.

FAUSTUS. O, might I see hell, and return again,
How happy were I then!

LUCIFER. Thou shalt; I will send for thee at midnight.
In meantime take this book; peruse it throughly,
And thou shalt turn thyself into what shape thou wilt.

FAUSTUS. Great thanks, mighty Lucifer!
This will I keep as chary as my life.

LUCIFER. Farewell, Faustus, and think on the devil.

FAUSTUS. Farewell, great Lucifer.

 [Exeunt LUCIFER and BELZEBUB.]

Come, Mephistophilis.

 [Exeunt.]

  Enter CHORUS.

CHORUS. Learned Faustus,
To know the secrets of astronomy
Graven in the book of Jove's high firmament,
Did mount himself to scale Olympus' top,
Being seated in a chariot burning bright,
Drawn by the strength of yoky dragons' necks.
He now is gone to prove cosmography,
And, as I guess, will first arrive at Rome,

To see the Pope and manner of his court,
And take some part of holy Peter's feast,
That to this day is highly solemniz'd.
   [Exit.]
     Enter FAUSTUS and MEPHISTOPHILIS.
   FAUSTUS. Having now, my good Mephistophilis,
Pass'd with delight the stately town of Trier,
Environ'd round with airy mountain-tops,
With walls of flint, and deep-entrenched lakes,
Not to be won by any conquering prince;
From Paris next, coasting the realm of France,
We saw the river Maine fall into Rhine,
Whose banks are set with groves of fruitful vines;
Then up to Naples, rich Campania,
Whose buildings fair and gorgeous to the eye,
The streets straight forth, and pav'd with finest brick,
Quarter the town in four equivalents:
There saw we learned Maro's golden tomb,
The way he cut, an English mile in length,
Thorough a rock of stone, in one night's space;
From thence to Venice, Padua, and the rest,
In one of which a sumptuous temple stands,
That threats the stars with her aspiring top.
Thus hitherto hath Faustus spent his time:
But tell me now what resting-place is this?
Hast thou, as erst I did command,
Conducted me within the walls of Rome?
   MEPHIST. Faustus, I have; and, because we will not be unprovided,
I have taken up his Holiness' privy-chamber for our use.
   FAUSTUS. I hope his Holiness will bid us welcome.
   MEPHIST.
Tut, 'tis no matter; man; we'll be bold with his good cheer.
And now, my Faustus, that thou mayst perceive
What Rome containeth to delight thee with,
Know that this city stands upon seven hills
That underprop the groundwork of the same:
Just through the midst runs flowing Tiber's stream
With winding banks that cut it in two parts;
Over the which four stately bridges lean,

That make safe passage to each part of Rome:
Upon the bridge call'd Ponte Angelo
Erected is a castle passing strong,
Within whose walls such store of ordnance are,
And double cannons fram'd of carved brass,
As match the days within one complete year;
Besides the gates, and high pyramides,
Which Julius Caesar brought from Africa.

    FAUSTUS. Now, by the kingdoms of infernal rule,
Of Styx, of Acheron, and the fiery lake
Of ever-burning Phlegethon, I swear
That I do long to see the monuments
And situation of bright-splendent Rome:
Come, therefore, let's away.

    MEPHIST. Nay, Faustus, stay: I know you'd fain see the Pope,
And take some part of holy Peter's feast,
Where thou shalt see a troop of bald-pate friars,
Whose summum bonum is in belly-cheer.

    FAUSTUS. Well, I'm content to compass then some sport,
And by their folly make us merriment.
Then charm me, that I
May be invisible, to do what I please,
Unseen of any whilst I stay in Rome.

    [Mephistophilis charms him.]

    MEPHIST. So, Faustus; now
Do what thou wilt, thou shalt not be discern'd.

      Sound a Sonnet. Enter the POPE and the CARDINAL OF
    LORRAIN to the banquet, with FRIARS attending.

    POPE. My Lord of Lorrain, will't please you draw near?

    FAUSTUS. Fall to, and the devil choke you, an you spare!

    POPE. How now! who's that which spake?—Friars, look about.

    FIRST FRIAR. Here's nobody, if it like your Holiness.

    POPE. My lord, here is a dainty dish was sent me from the Bishop
of Milan.

    FAUSTUS. I thank you, sir.

    [Snatches the dish.]

    POPE. How now! who's that which snatched the meat from me? will
no man look?—My lord, this dish was sent me from the Cardinal
of Florence.

FAUSTUS. You say true; I'll ha't.

[Snatches the dish.]

POPE. What, again!—My lord, I'll drink to your grace.

FAUSTUS. I'll pledge your grace.

[Snatches the cup.]

C. OF LOR. My lord, it may be some ghost, newly crept out of
Purgatory, come to beg a pardon of your Holiness.

POPE. It may be so.—Friars, prepare a dirge to lay the fury
of this ghost.—Once again, my lord, fall to.

[The POPE crosses himself.]

FAUSTUS. What, are you crossing of yourself?
Well, use that trick no more, I would advise you.

[The POPE crosses himself again.]

Well, there's the second time. Aware the third;
I give you fair warning.

[The POPE crosses himself again, and FAUSTUS hits him a box
of the ear; and they all run away.]

Come on, Mephistophilis; what shall we do?

MEPHIST. Nay, I know not: we shall be cursed with bell, book,
and candle.

FAUSTUS. How! bell, book, and candle,—candle, book, and bell,—
Forward and backward, to curse Faustus to hell!
Anon you shall hear a hog grunt, a calf bleat, and an ass bray,
Because it is Saint Peter's holiday.

Re-enter all the FRIARS to sing the Dirge.

FIRST FRIAR.

Come, brethren, let's about our business with good devotion.

They sing.

CURSED BE HE THAT STOLE AWAY HIS HOLINESS' MEAT
FROM THE
TABLE! maledicat Dominus!
CURSED BE HE THAT STRUCK HIS HOLINESS A BLOW ON THE
FACE!
maledicat Dominus!
CURSED BE HE THAT TOOK FRIAR SANDELO A BLOW ON THE
PATE!
maledicat Dominus!
CURSED BE HE THAT DISTURBETH OUR HOLY DIRGE! maledicat
Dominus!

CURSED BE HE THAT TOOK AWAY HIS HOLINESS' WINE!
maledicat
   Dominus? ['?' sic]
     Et omnes Sancti! Amen!
       [MEPHISTOPHILIS and FAUSTUS beat the FRIARS, and fling
      fire-works among them; and so exeunt.]
      Enter CHORUS.
   CHORUS. When Faustus had with pleasure ta'en the view
Of rarest things, and royal courts of kings,
He stay'd his course, and so returned home;
Where such as bear his absence but with grief,
I mean his friends and near'st companions,
Did gratulate his safety with kind words,
And in their conference of what befell,
Touching his journey through the world and air,
They put forth questions of astrology,
Which Faustus answer'd with such learned skill
As they admir'd and wonder'd at his wit.
Now is his fame spread forth in every land:
Amongst the rest the Emperor is one,
Carolus the Fifth, at whose palace now
Faustus is feasted 'mongst his noblemen.
What there he did, in trial of his art,
I leave untold; your eyes shall see['t] perform'd.
    [Exit.]
      Enter ROBIN the Ostler, with a book in his hand.
   ROBIN. O, this is admirable! here I ha' stolen one of Doctor
Faustus' conjuring-books, and, i'faith, I mean to search some
circles for my own use. Now will I make all the maidens in our
parish dance at my pleasure, stark naked, before me; and so
by that means I shall see more than e'er I felt or saw yet.
     Enter RALPH, calling ROBIN.
   RALPH. Robin, prithee, come away; there's a gentleman tarries
to have his horse, and he would have his things rubbed and made
clean: he keeps such a chafing with my mistress about it; and
she has sent me to look thee out; prithee, come away.
   ROBIN. Keep out, keep out, or else you are blown up, you are
dismembered, Ralph: keep out, for I am about a roaring piece
of work.

RALPH. Come, what doest thou with that same book? thou canst
not read?

ROBIN. Yes, my master and mistress shall find that I can read,
he for his forehead, she for her private study; she's born to
bear with me, or else my art fails.

RALPH. Why, Robin, what book is that?

ROBIN. What book! why, the most intolerable book for conjuring
that e'er was invented by any brimstone devil.

RALPH. Canst thou conjure with it?

ROBIN. I can do all these things easily with it; first, I can
make thee drunk with ippocras at any tabern in Europe
for nothing; that's one of my conjuring works.

RALPH. Our Master Parson says that's nothing.

ROBIN. True, Ralph: and more, Ralph, if thou hast any mind to
Nan Spit, our kitchen-maid, then turn her and wind her to thy own
use, as often as thou wilt, and at midnight.

RALPH. O, brave, Robin! shall I have Nan Spit, and to mine own
use? On that condition I'll feed thy devil with horse-bread as
long as he lives, of free cost.

ROBIN. No more, sweet Ralph: let's go and make clean our boots,
which lie foul upon our hands, and then to our conjuring in the
devil's name.

[Exeunt.]

　　Enter ROBIN and RALPH with a silver goblet.

ROBIN. Come, Ralph: did not I tell thee, we were for ever made
by this Doctor Faustus' book? ecce, signum! here's a simple
purchase for horse-keepers: our horses shall eat no hay as
long as this lasts.

RALPH. But, Robin, here comes the Vintner.

ROBIN. Hush! I'll gull him supernaturally.

　　Enter VINTNER.

Drawer, I hope all is paid; God be with you!—Come, Ralph.

VINTNER. Soft, sir; a word with you. I must yet have a goblet paid
from you, ere you go.

ROBIN. I a goblet, Ralph, I a goblet!—I scorn you; and you are
but a, &c. I a goblet! search me.

VINTNER. I mean so, sir, with your favour.

[Searches ROBIN.]

ROBIN. How say you now?

VINTNER. I must say somewhat to your fellow.—You, sir!

RALPH. Me, sir! me, sir! search your fill. [VINTNER searches him.]
Now, sir, you may be ashamed to burden honest men with a matter
of truth.

VINTNER. Well, tone of you hath this goblet about you.

ROBIN. You lie, drawer, 'tis afore me [Aside].—Sirrah you, I'll
teach you to impeach honest men;—stand by;—I'll scour you for
a goblet;—stand aside you had best, I charge you in the name of
Belzebub.—Look to the goblet, Ralph [Aside to RALPH].

VINTNER. What mean you, sirrah?

ROBIN. I'll tell you what I mean. [Reads from a book] Sanctobulorum
Periphrasticon—nay, I'll tickle you, Vintner.—Look to the goblet,
Ralph [Aside to RALPH].—[Reads] Polypragmos Belseborams framanto
pacostiphos tostu, Mephistophilis, &c.

Enter MEPHISTOPHILIS, sets squibs at their backs, and then
exit. They run about.

VINTNER. O, nomine Domini! what meanest thou, Robin? thou hast
no
goblet.

RALPH. Peccatum peccatorum!—Here's thy goblet, good Vintner.
[Gives the goblet to VINTNER, who exit.]

ROBIN. Misericordia pro nobis! what shall I do? Good devil, forgive
me now, and I'll never rob thy library more.

Re-enter MEPHISTOPHILIS.

MEPHIST. Monarch of Hell, under whose black survey
Great potentates do kneel with awful fear,
Upon whose altars thousand souls do lie,
How am I vexed with these villains' charms?
From Constantinople am I hither come,
Only for pleasure of these damned slaves.

ROBIN. How, from Constantinople! you have had a great journey:
will you take sixpence in your purse to pay for your supper, and
be gone?

MEPHIST. Well, villains, for your presumption, I transform thee
into an ape, and thee into a dog; and so be gone!
[Exit.]

ROBIN. How, into an ape! that's brave: I'll have fine sport with
the boys; I'll get nuts and apples enow.

RALPH. And I must be a dog.

ROBIN. I'faith, thy head will never be out of the pottage-pot.
[Exeunt.]

Enter EMPEROR, FAUSTUS, and a KNIGHT, with ATTEN-
DANTS.

EMPEROR. Master Doctor Faustus, I have heard strange report
of thy knowledge in the black art, how that none in my empire
nor in the whole world can compare with thee for the rare effects
of magic: they say thou hast a familiar spirit, by whom thou canst
accomplish what thou list. This, therefore, is my request, that
thou let me see some proof of thy skill, that mine eyes may be
witnesses to confirm what mine ears have heard reported: and here
I swear to thee, by the honour of mine imperial crown, that,
whatever thou doest, thou shalt be no ways prejudiced or endamaged.

KNIGHT. I'faith, he looks much like a conjurer.
[Aside.]

FAUSTUS. My gracious sovereign, though I must confess myself far
inferior to the report men have published, and nothing answerable
to the honour of your imperial majesty, yet, for that love and duty
binds me thereunto, I am content to do whatsoever your majesty
shall command me.

EMPEROR. Then, Doctor Faustus, mark what I shall say.
As I was sometime solitary set
Within my closet, sundry thoughts arose
About the honour of mine ancestors,
How they had won by prowess such exploits,
Got such riches, subdu'd so many kingdoms,
As we that do succeed, or they that shall
Hereafter possess our throne, shall
(I fear me) ne'er attain to that degree
Of high renown and great authority:
Amongst which kings is Alexander the Great,
Chief spectacle of the world's pre-eminence,
The bright shining of whose glorious acts
Lightens the world with his reflecting beams,
As when I hear but motion made of him,
It grieves my soul I never saw the man:
If, therefore, thou, by cunning of thine art,
Canst raise this man from hollow vaults below,
Where lies entomb'd this famous conqueror,

And bring with him his beauteous paramour,
Both in their right shapes, gesture, and attire
They us'd to wear during their time of life,
Thou shalt both satisfy my just desire,
And give me cause to praise thee whilst I live.

FAUSTUS. My gracious lord, I am ready to accomplish your request, so far forth as by art and power of my spirit I am able to perform.

KNIGHT. I'faith, that's just nothing at all.

[Aside.]

FAUSTUS. But, if it like your grace, it is not in my ability to present before your eyes the true substantial bodies of those two deceased princes, which long since are consumed to dust.

KNIGHT. Ay, marry, Master Doctor, now there's a sign of grace in you, when you will confess the truth.

[Aside.]

FAUSTUS. But such spirits as can lively resemble Alexander and his paramour shall appear before your grace, in that manner that they both lived in, in their most flourishing estate; which I doubt not shall sufficiently content your imperial majesty.

EMPEROR. Go to, Master Doctor; let me see them presently.

KNIGHT. Do you hear, Master Doctor? you bring Alexander and his paramour before the Emperor!

FAUSTUS. How then, sir?

KNIGHT. I'faith, that's as true as Diana turned me to a stag.

FAUSTUS. No, sir; but, when Actaeon died, he left the horns for you.—Mephistophilis, be gone.

[Exit MEPHISTOPHILIS.]

KNIGHT. Nay, an you go to conjuring, I'll be gone.

[Exit.]

FAUSTUS. I'll meet with you anon for interrupting me so.
—Here they are, my gracious lord.

       Re-enter MEPHISTOPHILIS with SPIRITS in the shapes of ALEXANDER
      and his PARAMOUR.

EMPEROR. Master Doctor, I heard this lady, while she lived, had a wart or mole in her neck: how shall I know whether it be so or no?

FAUSTUS. Your highness may boldly go and see.

EMPEROR. Sure, these are no spirits, but the true substantial bodies of those two deceased princes.

[Exeunt Spirits.]

FAUSTUS. Wilt please your highness now to send for the knight
that was so pleasant with me here of late?

EMPEROR. One of you call him forth.

[Exit ATTENDANT.]

Re-enter the KNIGHT with a pair of horns on his head.

How now, sir knight! why, I had thought thou hadst been a bachelor,
but now I see thou hast a wife, that not only gives thee horns,
but makes thee wear them. Feel on thy head.

KNIGHT. Thou damned wretch and execrable dog,
Bred in the concave of some monstrous rock,
How dar'st thou thus abuse a gentleman?
Villain, I say, undo what thou hast done!

FAUSTUS. O, not so fast, sir! there's no haste: but, good, are
you remembered how you crossed me in my conference with the
Emperor? I think I have met with you for it.

EMPEROR. Good Master Doctor, at my entreaty release him: he hath
done penance sufficient.

FAUSTUS. My gracious lord, not so much for the injury he offered
me here in your presence, as to delight you with some mirth, hath
Faustus worthily requited this injurious knight; which being all
I desire, I am content to release him of his horns:—and,
sir knight, hereafter speak well of scholars.—Mephistophilis,
transform him straight. [MEPHISTOPHILIS removes the horns.]
—Now, my good lord, having done my duty, I humbly take my leave.

EMPEROR. Farewell, Master Doctor: yet, ere you go,
Expect from me a bounteous reward.

[Exeunt EMPEROR, KNIGHT, and ATTENDANTS.]

FAUSTUS. Now, Mephistophilis, the restless course
That time doth run with calm and silent foot,
Shortening my days and thread of vital life,
Calls for the payment of my latest years:
Therefore, sweet Mephistophilis, let us
Make haste to Wertenberg.

MEPHIST. What, will you go on horse-back or on foot[?]

FAUSTUS. Nay, till I'm past this fair and pleasant green,
I'll walk on foot.

Enter a HORSE-COURSER.

HORSE-COURSER. I have been all this day seeking one Master
Fustian:
mass, see where he is!—God save you, Master Doctor!

FAUSTUS. What, horse-courser! you are well met.

HORSE-COURSER. Do you hear, sir? I have brought you forty dollars
for your horse.

FAUSTUS. I cannot sell him so: if thou likest him for fifty, take
him.

HORSE-COURSER. Alas, sir, I have no more!—I pray you, speak for
me.

MEPHIST. I pray you, let him have him: he is an honest fellow,
and he has a great charge, neither wife nor child.

FAUSTUS. Well, come, give me your money [HORSE-COURSER
gives
FAUSTUS the money]: my boy will deliver him to you. But I must
tell you one thing before you have him; ride him not into the
water, at any hand.

HORSE-COURSER. Why, sir, will he not drink of all waters?

FAUSTUS. O, yes, he will drink of all waters; but ride him not
into the water: ride him over hedge or ditch, or where thou wilt,
but not into the water.

HORSE-COURSER. Well, sir.—Now am I made man for ever: I'll not
leave my horse for forty: if he had but the quality of
hey-ding-ding, hey-ding-ding, I'd make a brave living on him:
he has a buttock as slick as an eel [Aside].—Well, God b'wi'ye,
sir: your boy will deliver him me: but, hark you, sir; if my horse
be sick or ill at ease, if I bring his water to you, you'll tell
me what it is?

FAUSTUS. Away, you villain! what, dost think I am a horse-doctor?
[Exit HORSE-COURSER.]
What art thou, Faustus, but a man condemn'd to die?
Thy fatal time doth draw to final end;
Despair doth drive distrust into my thoughts:
Confound these passions with a quiet sleep:
Tush, Christ did call the thief upon the Cross;
Then rest thee, Faustus, quiet in conceit.
[Sleeps in his chair.]
Re-enter HORSE-COURSER, all wet, crying.
HORSE-COURSER. Alas, alas! Doctor Fustian, quoth a? mass, Doctor

Lopus was never such a doctor: has given me a purgation, has
purged me of forty dollars; I shall never see them more. But yet,
like an ass as I was, I would not be ruled by him, for he bade me
I should ride him into no water: now I, thinking my horse had had
some rare quality that he would not have had me know of, I,
like a venturous youth, rid him into the deep pond at the town's
end. I was no sooner in the middle of the pond, but my horse
vanished away, and I sat upon a bottle of hay, never so near
drowning in my life. But I'll seek out my doctor, and have my
forty dollars again, or I'll make it the dearest horse!—O,
yonder is his snipper-snapper.—Do you hear? you, hey-pass,
where's your master?

    MEPHIST. Why, sir, what would you? you cannot speak with him.

    HORSE-COURSER. But I will speak with him.

    MEPHIST. Why, he's fast asleep: come some other time.

    HORSE-COURSER. I'll speak with him now, or I'll break his
glass-windows about his ears.

    MEPHIST. I tell thee, he has not slept this eight nights.

    HORSE-COURSER. An he have not slept this eight weeks, I'll
speak with him.

    MEPHIST. See, where he is, fast asleep.

    HORSE-COURSER. Ay, this is he.—God save you, Master Doctor,
Master Doctor, Master Doctor Fustian! forty dollars, forty dollars
for a bottle of hay!

    MEPHIST. Why, thou seest he hears thee not.

    HORSE-COURSER. So-ho, ho! so-ho, ho! [Hollows in his ear.] No,
will you not wake? I'll make you wake ere I go. [Pulls FAUSTUS
by the leg, and pulls it away.] Alas, I am undone! what shall
I do?

    FAUSTUS. O, my leg, my leg!—Help, Mephistophilis! call the
officers.—My leg, my leg!

    MEPHIST. Come, villain, to the constable.

    HORSE-COURSER. O Lord, sir, let me go, and I'll give you forty
dollars more!

    MEPHIST. Where be they?

    HORSE-COURSER. I have none about me: come to my ostry,
and I'll give them you.

    MEPHIST. Be gone quickly.

    [HORSE-COURSER runs away.]

FAUSTUS. What, is he gone? farewell he! Faustus has his leg again, and the Horse-courser, I take it, a bottle of hay for his labour: well, this trick shall cost him forty dollars more.

Enter WAGNER.

How now, Wagner! what's the news with thee?

WAGNER. Sir, the Duke of Vanholt doth earnestly entreat your company.

FAUSTUS. The Duke of Vanholt! an honourable gentleman, to whom I must be no niggard of my cunning.—Come, Mephistophilis, let's away to him.

[Exeunt.]

Enter the DUKE OF VANHOLT, the DUCHESS, and FAUSTUS.

DUKE. Believe me, Master Doctor, this merriment hath much pleased me.

FAUSTUS. My gracious lord, I am glad it contents you so well. —But it may be, madam, you take no delight in this. I have heard that great-bellied women do long for some dainties or other: what is it, madam? tell me, and you shall have it.

DUCHESS. Thanks, good Master Doctor: and, for I see your courteous intent to pleasure me, I will not hide from you the thing my heart desires; and, were it now summer, as it is January and the dead time of the winter, I would desire no better meat than a dish of ripe grapes.

FAUSTUS. Alas, madam, that's nothing!—Mephistophilis, be gone. [Exit MEPHISTOPHILIS.] Were it a greater thing than this, so it would content you, you should have it.

Re-enter MEPHISTOPHILIS with grapes.

Here they be, madam: wilt please you taste on them?

DUKE. Believe me, Master Doctor, this makes me wonder above the rest, that being in the dead time of winter and in the month of January, how you should come by these grapes.

FAUSTUS. If it like your grace, the year is divided into two circles over the whole world, that, when it is here winter with us, in the contrary circle it is summer with them, as in India, Saba, and farther countries in the east; and by means of a swift spirit that I have, I had them brought hither, as you see. —How do you like them, madam? be they good?

DUCHESS. Believe me, Master Doctor, they be the best grapes that e'er I tasted in my life before.

FAUSTUS. I am glad they content you so, madam.

DUKE. Come, madam, let us in, where you must well reward this learned man for the great kindness he hath shewed to you.

DUCHESS. And so I will, my lord; and, whilst I live, rest beholding for this courtesy.

FAUSTUS. I humbly thank your grace.

DUKE. Come, Master Doctor, follow us, and receive your reward.

[Exeunt.]

Enter WAGNER.

WAGNER. I think my master means to die shortly,
For he hath given to me all his goods:
And yet, methinks, if that death were near,
He would not banquet, and carouse, and swill
Amongst the students, as even now he doth,
Who are at supper with such belly-cheer
As Wagner ne'er beheld in all his life.
See, where they come! belike the feast is ended.

[Exit.]

Enter FAUSTUS with two or three SCHOLARS, and MEPHISTOPHILIS.

FIRST SCHOLAR. Master Doctor Faustus, since our conference about fair ladies, which was the beautifulest in all the world, we have determined with ourselves that Helen of Greece was the admirablest lady that ever lived: therefore, Master Doctor, if you will do us that favour, as to let us see that peerless dame of Greece, whom all the world admires for majesty, we should think ourselves much beholding unto you.

FAUSTUS. Gentlemen,
For that I know your friendship is unfeign'd,
And Faustus' custom is not to deny
The just requests of those that wish him well,
You shall behold that peerless dame of Greece,
No otherways for pomp and majesty
Than when Sir Paris cross'd the seas with her,
And brought the spoils to rich Dardania.
Be silent, then, for danger is in words.

[Music sounds, and HELEN passeth over the stage.]

SECOND SCHOLAR. Too simple is my wit to tell her praise,
Whom all the world admires for majesty.

THIRD SCHOLAR. No marvel though the angry Greeks pursu'd
With ten years' war the rape of such a queen,
Whose heavenly beauty passeth all compare.
  FIRST SCHOLAR. Since we have seen the pride of Nature's works,
And only paragon of excellence,
Let us depart; and for this glorious deed
Happy and blest be Faustus evermore!
  FAUSTUS. Gentlemen, farewell: the same I wish to you.
    [Exeunt SCHOLARS.]
      Enter an OLD MAN.
    OLD MAN. Ah, Doctor Faustus, that I might prevail
To guide thy steps unto the way of life,
By which sweet path thou mayst attain the goal
That shall conduct thee to celestial rest!
Break heart, drop blood, and mingle it with tears,
Tears falling from repentant heaviness
Of thy most vile and loathsome filthiness,
The stench whereof corrupts the inward soul
With such flagitious crimes of heinous sin
As no commiseration may expel,
But mercy, Faustus, of thy Saviour sweet,
Whose blood alone must wash away thy guilt.
  FAUSTUS. Where art thou, Faustus? wretch, what hast thou done?
Damn'd art thou, Faustus, damn'd; despair and die!
Hell calls for right, and with a roaring voice
Says, "Faustus, come; thine hour is almost come;"
And Faustus now will come to do thee right.
    [MEPHISTOPHILIS gives him a dagger.]
    OLD MAN. Ah, stay, good Faustus, stay thy desperate steps!
I see an angel hovers o'er thy head,
And, with a vial full of precious grace,
Offers to pour the same into thy soul:
Then call for mercy, and avoid despair.
  FAUSTUS. Ah, my sweet friend, I feel
Thy words to comfort my distressed soul!
Leave me a while to ponder on my sins.
  OLD MAN. I go, sweet Faustus; but with heavy cheer,
Fearing the ruin of thy hopeless soul.
    [Exit.]

FAUSTUS. Accursed Faustus, where is mercy now?
I do repent; and yet I do despair:
Hell strives with grace for conquest in my breast:
What shall I do to shun the snares of death?

MEPHIST. Thou traitor, Faustus, I arrest thy soul
For disobedience to my sovereign lord:
Revolt, or I'll in piece-meal tear thy flesh.

FAUSTUS. Sweet Mephistophilis, entreat thy lord
To pardon my unjust presumption,
And with my blood again I will confirm
My former vow I made to Lucifer.

MEPHIST. Do it, then, quickly, with unfeigned heart,
Lest greater danger do attend thy drift.

FAUSTUS. Torment, sweet friend, that base and crooked age,
That durst dissuade me from thy Lucifer,
With greatest torments that our hell affords.

MEPHIST. His faith is great; I cannot touch his soul;
But what I may afflict his body with
I will attempt, which is but little worth.

FAUSTUS. One thing, good servant, let me crave of thee,
To glut the longing of my heart's desire,—
That I might have unto my paramour
That heavenly Helen which I saw of late,
Whose sweet embracings may extinguish clean
Those thoughts that do dissuade me from my vow,
And keep mine oath I made to Lucifer.

MEPHIST. Faustus, this, or what else thou shalt desire,
Shall be perform'd in twinkling of an eye.

    Re-enter HELEN.

FAUSTUS. Was this the face that launch'd a thousand ships,
And burnt the topless towers of Ilium—
Sweet Helen, make me immortal with a kiss.—

    [Kisses her.]

Her lips suck forth my soul: see, where it flies!—
Come, Helen, come, give me my soul again.
Here will I dwell, for heaven is in these lips,
And all is dross that is not Helena.
I will be Paris, and for love of thee,
Instead of Troy, shall Wertenberg be sack'd;

And I will combat with weak Menelaus,
And wear thy colours on my plumed crest;
Yea, I will wound Achilles in the heel,
And then return to Helen for a kiss.
O, thou art fairer than the evening air
Clad in the beauty of a thousand stars;
Brighter art thou than flaming Jupiter
When he appear'd to hapless Semele;
More lovely than the monarch of the sky
In wanton Arethusa's azur'd arms;
And none but thou shalt be my paramour!
    [Exeunt.]
      Enter the OLD MAN.
  OLD MAN. Accursed Faustus, miserable man,
That from thy soul exclud'st the grace of heaven,
And fly'st the throne of his tribunal-seat!
      Enter DEVILS.
  Satan begins to sift me with his pride:
As in this furnace God shall try my faith,
My faith, vile hell, shall triumph over thee.
Ambitious fiends, see how the heavens smile
At your repulse, and laugh your state to scorn!
Hence, hell! for hence I fly unto my God.
    [Exeunt,—on one side, DEVILS, on the other, OLD MAN.]
      Enter FAUSTUS, with SCHOLARS.
  FAUSTUS. Ah, gentlemen!
  FIRST SCHOLAR. What ails Faustus?
  FAUSTUS. Ah, my sweet chamber-fellow, had I lived with thee,
then had I lived still! but now I die eternally. Look, comes
he not? comes he not?
  SECOND SCHOLAR. What means Faustus?
  THIRD SCHOLAR. Belike he is grown into some sickness by being
over-solitary.
  FIRST SCHOLAR. If it be so, we'll have physicians to cure him.
—'Tis but a surfeit; never fear, man.
  FAUSTUS. A surfeit of deadly sin, that hath damned both body
and soul.
    SECOND SCHOLAR. Yet, Faustus, look up to heaven; remember
God's

mercies are infinite.

FAUSTUS. But Faustus' offence can ne'er be pardoned: the serpent that tempted Eve may be saved, but not Faustus. Ah, gentlemen, hear me with patience, and tremble not at my speeches! Though my heart pants and quivers to remember that I have been a student here these thirty years, O, would I had never seen Wertenberg, never read book! and what wonders I have done, all Germany can witness, yea, all the world; for which Faustus hath lost both Germany and the world, yea, heaven itself, heaven, the seat of God, the throne of the blessed, the kingdom of joy; and must remain in hell for ever, hell, ah, hell, for ever! Sweet friends, what shall become of Faustus, being in hell for ever?

THIRD SCHOLAR. Yet, Faustus, call on God.

FAUSTUS. On God, whom Faustus hath abjured! on God, whom Faustus

hath blasphemed! Ah, my God, I would weep! but the devil draws in my tears. Gush forth blood, instead of tears! yea, life and soul! O, he stays my tongue! I would lift up my hands; but see, they hold them, they hold them!

ALL. Who, Faustus?

FAUSTUS. Lucifer and Mephistophilis. Ah, gentlemen, I gave them my soul for my cunning!

ALL. God forbid!

FAUSTUS. God forbade it, indeed; but Faustus hath done it: for vain pleasure of twenty-four years hath Faustus lost eternal joy and felicity. I writ them a bill with mine own blood: the date is expired; the time will come, and he will fetch me.

FIRST SCHOLAR. Why did not Faustus tell us of this before, that divines might have prayed for thee?

FAUSTUS. Oft have I thought to have done so; but the devil threatened to tear me in pieces, if I named God, to fetch both body and soul, if I once gave ear to divinity: and now 'tis too late. Gentlemen, away, lest you perish with me.

SECOND SCHOLAR. O, what shall we do to save Faustus?

FAUSTUS. Talk not of me, but save yourselves, and depart.

THIRD SCHOLAR. God will strengthen me; I will stay with Faustus.

FIRST SCHOLAR. Tempt not God, sweet friend; but let us into the next room, and there pray for him.

FAUSTUS. Ay, pray for me, pray for me; and what noise soever ye hear, come not unto me, for nothing can rescue me.

SECOND SCHOLAR. Pray thou, and we will pray that God may have
mercy upon thee.

FAUSTUS. Gentlemen, farewell: if I live till morning, I'll visit
you; if not, Faustus is gone to hell.

ALL. Faustus, farewell.

[Exeunt SCHOLARS.—The clock strikes eleven.]

FAUSTUS. Ah, Faustus,
Now hast thou but one bare hour to live,
And then thou must be damn'd perpetually!
Stand still, you ever-moving spheres of heaven,
That time may cease, and midnight never come;
Fair Nature's eye, rise, rise again, and make
Perpetual day; or let this hour be but
A year, a month, a week, a natural day,
That Faustus may repent and save his soul!
O lente, lente currite, noctis equi!
The stars move still, time runs, the clock will strike,
The devil will come, and Faustus must be damn'd.
O, I'll leap up to my God!—Who pulls me down?—
See, see, where Christ's blood streams in the firmament!
One drop would save my soul, half a drop: ah, my Christ!—
Ah, rend not my heart for naming of my Christ!
Yet will I call on him: O, spare me, Lucifer!—
Where is it now? 'tis gone: and see, where God
Stretcheth out his arm, and bends his ireful brows!
Mountains and hills, come, come, and fall on me,
And hide me from the heavy wrath of God!
No, no!
Then will I headlong run into the earth:
Earth, gape! O, no, it will not harbour me!
You stars that reign'd at my nativity,
Whose influence hath allotted death and hell,
Now draw up Faustus, like a foggy mist.
Into the entrails of yon labouring cloud[s],
That, when you vomit forth into the air,
My limbs may issue from your smoky mouths,
So that my soul may but ascend to heaven!

[The clock strikes the half-hour.]

Ah, half the hour is past! 'twill all be past anon
O God,
If thou wilt not have mercy on my soul,
Yet for Christ's sake, whose blood hath ransom'd me,
Impose some end to my incessant pain;
Let Faustus live in hell a thousand years,
A hundred thousand, and at last be sav'd!
O, no end is limited to damned souls!
Why wert thou not a creature wanting soul?
Or why is this immortal that thou hast?
Ah, Pythagoras' metempsychosis, were that true,
This soul should fly from me, and I be chang'd
Unto some brutish beast! all beasts are happy,
For, when they die,
Their souls are soon dissolv'd in elements;
But mine must live still to be plagu'd in hell.
Curs'd be the parents that engender'd me!
No, Faustus, curse thyself, curse Lucifer
That hath depriv'd thee of the joys of heaven.
    [The clock strikes twelve.]
O, it strikes, it strikes! Now, body, turn to air,
Or Lucifer will bear thee quick to hell!
    [Thunder and lightning.]
O soul, be chang'd into little water-drops,
And fall into the ocean, ne'er be found!
      Enter DEVILS.
  My God, my god, look not so fierce on me!
Adders and serpents, let me breathe a while!
Ugly hell, gape not! come not, Lucifer!
I'll burn my books!—Ah, Mephistophilis!
   [Exeunt DEVILS with FAUSTUS.]
     Enter CHORUS.
  CHORUS. Cut is the branch that might have grown full straight,
And burned is Apollo's laurel-bough,
That sometime grew within this learned man.
Faustus is gone: regard his hellish fall,
Whose fiendful fortune may exhort the wise,
Only to wonder at unlawful things,
Whose deepness doth entice such forward wits

To practice more than heavenly power permits.
   [Exit.]
    Terminat hora diem; terminat auctor opus.

CPSIA information can be obtained
at www.ICGtesting.com
Printed in the USA
LVHW042135021221
705095LV00013B/2021